GENDER

· *Two Novellas in Verse* ·

GENDER

·*Two Novellas in Verse*·

⟨

Martin/Martina
&
Aftermath

ANNE HARDING WOODWORTH

atmosphere press

© 2022 Anne Harding Woodworth

Published by Atmosphere Press

ISBN: 978-1-63988-297-7

Cover design by Joseph Lledo

No part of this book may be reproduced without permission from the author except in brief quotations and in reviews.

atmospherepress.com

For my beloved Fred, who, thanks to his mother, recites poems from memory at the drop of a hat.

TABLE OF CONTENTS

Martin/Martina

Author's Note.	2
Cast of Characters	3
Prologue: From Mother Martina's View.	5
Martina's Father, Now a Widower, Breaks the News to His Daughter	9
Mother Martina Remembers the Vegetable Gardeners and Her Father's Death	12
The Artichokes' Lament	13
Mother Martina Remembers Father Ralph the Abbot, and the Artichoke Patch.	14
Brother Martin on His First Day with the Artichokes . . .	15
Brother Martin's Finger	16
The Innkeeper's Wife, a Jealous Mother, Speaks.	17
Bronwyn Scrutinizes Her Life at the Song of Flower . . .	19
The Innkeeper's Wife Speaks of the Vegetable Gardeners	20
The Artichoke Sonnets, Etc.	21
Bronwyn Reveals What Happened.	23
Bronwyn's Aria	24
Father Ralph Receives Three Returning Vegetable Gardeners	25
Father Ralph Receives the Innkeeper and His Wife . . .	26
Father Ralph Grieves for Brother Martin	28
Father Ralph Summons Brother Martin	29

Ralou Knows What to Do	30
Father Ralph Hands the Baby Over to Brother Martin	32
Martin Sets Off with the Infant	34
Father Ralph Reconsiders His Career	36
Martin's First Day as a Parent	37
Martin is a Mother/Father	38
Mother Martina Is Aware of the Sainthood Campaign	39
Mother Martina Alone at Night Thinks About Sainthood	40
Dino, Aged 7, Asks His Father for a Puppy	41
Mother Martina's First Posthumous Miracle	42
Mother Martina Focuses on Gender	44
Mother Martina Remembers Raising Dino	46
Martin Explains to Dino, Aged 12	47
Dino Absorbs What He Has Learned	48
Mother Martina Suspects She Has a Second Posthumous Miracle	49
Mother Martina Remembers the Day a Visitor Arrived at the Sentry House	51
Bronwyn Meets Dino, a Play	52
Dino Contemplates the News That He Has a Mother	53
Mother Martina Reminisces about Bronwyn's Arrival	54
Dino Asks About His Father	55
Mother Martina Is Grateful to Bronwyn	57
Mother Martina Thinks Back on the Day She Died	58
Mother Martina Has the Requisites for Sainthood	60
Mother Martina Hears the Good News, a Third Miracle	61
Epilogue: Ralou Mops the Floor of the Chapel	63

Aftermath

Author's Note.	68
Cast of Characters	69
Destruction.	71
The Fennel Men.	73
The Weavers and Their Cloth	75
The Builders	76
Weavers and Builders Together	78
Memory of Language	79
Memory of Sights	80
Building	82
Expulsion, the Beginning of Disintegration.	83
Escape.	85
Dying at a Loom in the Weaving Room	86
Burial of a Weaver	87
Stringing Beads for Relaxation	89
At Night at Home	91
Distrust	93
The Three Groups in Isolation	94
The Next Generation	96
On Even Footing: The End and the Beginning	98

MARTIN/MARTINA

ʅ

In a glass coffin, and silver,
in a chapel on an island,
here I lie
and have lain for nine hundred sixty years.

—Mother Martina

AUTHOR'S NOTE,
Martin/Martina

Martina, Brother Martin, Martin, Mother Martina, and Saint Martin/Martina are one and the same person. She was thought to be born female in the year 1000. When she was 16, she began to dress as a male and lived with her father on the close of a monastery. She dressed as a male until the day she died in 1063. It was only then that her gender was revealed.

Martin/Martina selflessly raised a child, not their own, from infancy. Upon their death, they were honored for this accomplishment by being laid in a glass coffin in a small island chapel, where we find them, or her, at the beginning of this tale.

In reading the verses that follow, the dates at the beginning of each are important to note. Time traverses back and forth between the 21st century, when the narrative is in the voice of Mother Martina, and the 11th century, when it moves into the voices of the other players in Mother Martina's life, including her young self.

CAST OF CHARACTERS

· in order of their appearance ·

Mother Martina
   (alternatively called Martina, Brother Martin, Martin, and St. Martin/Martina)

Martina's father, who becomes a monk

Brother William, a monk

The Artichokes, symbols of rejuvenation and long life, even in death

The Innkeeper's Wife, Bronwyn's mother

Bronwyn, daughter of the Innkeeper and his wife, birthmother of Dino

Father Ralph, abbot of the monastery

Ralou, who in the 11th century cares briefly for Dino and then for Mother Martina in the 21st

Dino, son of Bronwyn, raised by Martin

Rich Man, who finances Martin/Martina's sainthood

Rich Man's Wife

Eel Man, employee of Rich Man

· *Friday, August 26, 2022* ·

PROLOGUE: From Mother Martina's View

1
Women under black cloaks like crows' feathers
    whisper at my sides here. They peck around me,
peer through the glass of my coffin
    at the gold and green brocade I'm wearing,
    my soft-leather shoes unscuffed.
Silk gloves hide the gap of my missing finger,
    the one in a Topkapi case near St. John's hand,
though I've heard there was another in Corfu sold by a priest.
    In fact, I've heard he sold about thirteen of them.

2
I feel quite lovely now (it wasn't always so).
When I was dressing in a monk's tunic,
    so that I could stay with my father at the monastery,
I knew I did not make a handsome boy, or man,
    or girl/woman for that matter.
I was menstruating twice or thrice a year
and in the fifth year, my twentieth, not at all. Nothing
    bloomed. And breasts? None. Some might consider me
lucky. Hah! I remember the absence, but not with regret.

3
I think about becoming, dare I say it? a saint.
The old woman, Ralou, put the idea in my head.
    I usually laugh at what dear Ralou mumbles,
especially when she talks about me as a saint.
    But she doesn't hear me laughing,
just keeps on mopping the chapel floor
    or emptying vases of wilted flowers
    and talking to me as she goes about her work.
Well, sainthood, I must confess, does tempt me.
    It's an arduous road that many find unpaved and rutted,
    too rough to tread or cross in any seriousness.

4
I have recall that is perhaps destructive
>to my happiness. Yet joy is essential in the grave.

Memory calls forth events of my long life as a young person
>and later as a father/mother to my Dino.

I was never a wife to anyone, nor was I a husband. At times,
>I felt urges to be one or the other. I held it all within me.

Memory deepens acuity. Nothing is blurred.
>A disturbing clairvoyance now serves me well.

I can re-create scenes, characters, dialogs,
>and actualize conversations word for word—
>like the one I had with my father,

when he told me he was going to join a monastery.

5
Many conversations and stories I wasn't privy to
come to me and I can speak them
because I know how they went.
I re-create them, as I lie here, set them in their very years.
Perhaps it's this inactivity here in a glass case
from one century to another that's made my mind
>fulfill itself in creative memory.

6
But I am getting ahead of myself.
The artichokes knew
>what the monks were up to, knew
>what Father Ralph was thinking, knew
>what evil the Song of Flower innkeeper's wife was
>>brewing.

7
The spirit of the Innkeeper's daughter is with me even now—
>beautiful Bronwyn, misshapen and halt—I protect her
>>spirit,
>protect it still against the malevolence of her mother.

Progenitor is never the issue. Parent is.
Again, I am ahead of my story.

8
I was nobody, expelled from the close.
Somehow circulation of my tale—
      being father to my boy Dino—
began among the faithful, which is how
      I ended up in this glass coffin.
I was known and beatified for what I'd done to raise my boy.
Men and women through the centuries have known my story,
      the full meaning of which revealed itself upon my death.
Throughout my life, they never knew I was not his father.
I was not his mother either.

9

Visitors come into this chapel to see me, often widows in black
      or young girls with afflictions of one kind or another.
They leave flowers on top of my glass coffin.
Sometimes the women who look on me cry,
    and sometimes I cry when I hear them, or even when I'm
      alone.
I seem to promise equally fertility and infertility. Femininity
    and masculinity.
Some young women kneel beside my coffin asking for a child.
        Others weep out of fear there will be a child.
      I try to do what I can for them.

10

Ralou busies herself here in the chapel cleaning up after the visitors,
not hiding her disdain for their muddy shoes
      or the crumbs that drop from their pockets.
She welcomes the arrival of lone men, who kneel by my side.
She eavesdrops on their prayers. Lone men, she says,
      are tentative, reflective.
They grapple with hard truths, she says.

11
But she has contempt for the groups of men who visit.
> They wear caps and smell of fresh-water eel and wine.

They are cocky, nudge one another elbow to ribcage
> and slur their words to cover up what they fear I'll hear.

They light cigarettes that stifle the chortling in their maws,
> and they think the thoughts of adolescent boys:
> "What was he/she like under covers in the dark?"

Men are curious about how a woman makes love.
Men are curious about how a man makes love with another man.
And when the other man turns out to be a woman, or part-man part-woman,
> *all* men and women are curious.

The artichokes know.

· *Tuesday, June 21, 1016* ·

Martina's Father, Now a Widower, Breaks the News to His Daughter

Martina, my daughter,
you are of age now. I must go.

> *Where to, Father?*

To the monastery to save my soul through prayer.
I will devote myself to a god until my path becomes ocean.

> *What will become of me?*

I'll give you all my money and goods.
You will marry.
You will have children.
It is a parent's duty
to push the child out into a place of safety.

> *But my mother pushed me out*
> *long before there was any safety . . .*

. . . yes, too early, my child.
But no one can predict survival's limit.
Your mother didn't survive.
Miracles rarely happen during plague.

> *But Father, you say you're going to save your soul.*
> *What about mine?*

I can't save anyone else's. Not even yours.
I can save only life. Soul is other work,
beyond blood, muscle, rain, soil, gardens.
It seeks cold walls of solitude,
even within marriage and routine,
but I have not the first
and soon will have varied the latter.

> *I'm coming with you, Father.*
> *I am your home. I am your routine.*

You must remain and protect those who will be needing you.

> *No one needs me.*

Someone will, as yet unborn, even unconceived.

> *There will always be the unconceived in me.*

Ah, Martina, spoken like the adolescent you are.

> *I speak the truth of barren women and sterile men.*
> *I'm going where you are going, Father.*

I'm going to the monastery.
There are no women there.

> *Then I'll be a man.*

Already you are becoming a woman,
and the monks will not welcome you.

> *Tell me, Father, do I look like a woman*
> *with this chest as flat as any man's?*

Why, Martina, you are young yet. Oh, child, this is women's talk.
Where is your mother? Why did she succumb to the plague,
why did she leave you?

> *Father, I am old enough to know*
> *I do not follow a common path.*

You are impatient, Martina, impatient to become a woman.

> *That I am not. I have few rags to bury in the dead of night.*
> *Surely you have noticed my body does not follow the*
> *moon.*

Ah, but the moon goes by quarters and halves, as voices become
what they are to be. Monks sing matins in low bass tones.
Your voice is high and lovely.

    I can growl, Father.

All right, come then, child. You are persistent.
I'll cut your brown curls. Put on this tunic.
Growl, my girl/my son.

· *Monday, August 29, 2022* ·

Mother Martina Remembers the Vegetable Gardeners and Her Father's Death

Monastery life appealed to me.
I found gender of no personal
consequence. It was a joy
to be left inside myself.
Perhaps I felt that even more
than the Brothers, whose duty, they felt,
was to work and pray and meditate.

The vegetable gardeners
unlike the other Brothers
had to walk miles to their garden.
Maybe that is why they seemed
so unpleasant and resentful.
They worked two or three days at a time
and stayed at an inn, The Song of Flower.
Other gardeners, like my father and me,
remained within the monastery walls
to tend the gardens of the close.

The vegetable gardeners ignored me
while my father was alive. But I knew
they were not to be trusted.
And when my father died, I shed my tears
in dark corners, where the Brothers
would not hear my feminine weeping.

During the interment next to the monastery,
a vegetable gardener, Brother William,
whispered: "Now for some heavy work, my pet,"
and he flicked his tongue into my ear.
"Pretty little eunuch," he said *sotto voce*.

· Sunday, June 10, 1016 ·

The Artichokes' Lament

Bully-tyrants' havoc
reeks
oleaginous.
Gardener's
tunic
reeks.
Besmirched
soil
desiccated
wreaks
bully-tyrants' havoc.

· Wednesday, August 31, 2022 ·

Mother Martina Remembers Father Ralph the Abbot and the Artichoke Patch

After my father died, with secrecy's loneliness
in my grieving heart, Father Ralph, who seemed
to have a sense of me, called me into the rectory.

As he often did, perhaps out of embarrassment,
perhaps because he craved formal construct in his life,
spoke in rhyme:

> "Martin, heavy work, it's time!
> To the vegetables, my boy, to lime.
> The artichokes are dying of thirst.
> The drought, the weather's at its worst."

I thanked him for this opportunity
to continue working the earth
that held my father now,

work I found becalming and serene,
especially my job tending artichokes.

· *Tuesday, June 10, 1018*·

Brother Martin on His First Day with the Artichokes

Artichokes have a way of laughing at us Brothers
in a patch of weeds and stony soil.

They were in a sorry state this morning,
almost dead yet still merry-looking in their plot.

The Brothers didn't laugh but sourly toiled
'til they gave up trying to save the prickly plants

and left to take a snooze behind an oak,
while I just went on working the chokes back to life.

As I cut back some errant leaves, my knife slipped
and cut my finger, cut it worse than cut, cut

my finger off—which fell into the dirt. The stump
bled, but not so much as might be thought.

What blood there was, mixed its moisture
with the feeble artichokes.

· *Tuesday, June 17, 1018* ·

Brother Martin's Finger

Within a day, the flow of blood subsided.
Soon all pain was gone. The Innkeeper's wife
reluctantly gave me gauze.

The Brothers, who saw the accident
from behind the oak tree where they lolled,
pretended not to have seen it at all.

But I know for a fact that they went back
to the artichoke patch to locate
the severed finger sometime during the week.

Such a finger can demand a high price,
especially if they say it is a holy man's.

I don't care.

The finger has done its job. The artichokes
thrive, and I have learned that blood, bone,
and flesh, the stuff of gardening,

can make a plant—an artichoke or a rose—
prosper where I never knew they could.

· *Tuesday, January 6, 1019* ·

The Innkeeper's Wife, a Jealous Mother, Speaks

My daughter Bronwyn matures in sun and clay,
with crooked feet and curvèd back,
projects a look of hunch.

I used to hide her, used to wish for a cliff
to throw her over or a piper
who'd lead her out of my life.

My husband isn't her father, the old cuckold.
Bronwyn doesn't know the truth either.
She's a silent girl, never yearns

for things that girls desire—
pretty cottons, shiny hair,
boys, a kiss or two.

Her silence saddens my Innkeeper husband,
who speaks often of her beauty,
though never of mine.

He doesn't want to see that Bronwyn is
a girl defective and without
a pretty face, or grace.

I hear him tell her bawdy jokes and such
about the fools who fall into
rich men's cesspools.

I hear him tell her about false pregnancies,
shepherds, and animals. And Bronwyn giggles.
I hate to hear her laugh.

He lets her swallow the ale left in the bottom
of tankards by our customers.
The girl straightens her back.

He cries real tears to see her rectify
her posture, so I tell him to
get ahold of himself.

A man in a weeping state—blubbering, too,
crying like a woman for Chrissake—
is a perfect dolt.

And in the morning, after these wretched evenings,
Bronwyn wakes up curved, twisted,
ugly and buckled again,

and I thank God that a normal life has come
back to my home of the bargain.
I'm still the prettiest in the garden.

· *Tuesday, January 20, 1019* ·

Bronwyn Scrutinizes Her Life at the Song of Flower

>My mother wants to be
>prettier than me.
>She is, of course,
>prettier than me.
>She tries to keep me
>hidden. My twisted feet,
>my curving spine
>embarrass her into anger.

* * * * *

At night, my father, after he's closed
the Song, sometimes holds my hand
to steady me. He lets me drink ale left
in the bottom of the monks' and soldiers' cups.
He tells me jokes that make me laugh.

Laughing relaxes muscles, smooths
the face of tight and knotted wires
that shoot pain clear down my neck
into my back—during day-light hours—
across my shoulder and into my arm.

My father looks at me those nights
that I am laughing. It's as if
he's having a vision—I wonder
of what—of a healthy daughter?
in a different time and place?

These are quiet moments for me.
He takes my face into his hands
and kisses my brow.

· *Wednesday, April 12, 1021* ·

The Innkeeper's Wife Speaks of the Vegetable Gardeners

The Brothers work vegetables on into night,
too late to walk home at that dark hour.
So they come to our inn, for a few pints of ale,
something nourishing to eat. And a bed.

Often they ask me to please wash their feet,
which I do for the love of God,
and then I ask them to please wash mine,
which they do when the sun's gone down.

No foot-washing for soldiers, unless they're bleeding.
Occasional merchants come through the door,
and troubadours, fiddlers, their cheeks flushed,
and all of them keep their boots on in bed.

Romping with monks and washing their feet
makes me feel young and pretty,
gives me some fun. The monks think so, too—
except for Martin, not a real Brother,

though he does work wonders—or so I've heard—
with the artichokes, even though that first year
they snapped a finger off his delicate hand.

He looks like no one I've ever known,
not woman, mother, monk or other,
and never did he ever wince with pain.

· *Thursday, April 13, 1021* ·

The Artichoke Sonnets, Etc.

Six of us plants in the garden we stood
(the garden is miles away from the close).
We wouldn't sprout a sucker or bud—
of one mind we were, rebellion our mode
against unkind monks who'd poke us with rakes,
stab us with axes and nick us with hoes,
tie us tight to rotten wood stakes,
keep water from reaching our sickly roots.
Decapitation were threats so profound,
we trembled and crackled when monks were around.
We withered, reduced to unseemly fare.
We bent our parched necks toward the depths of the earth
(we're never too pretty with even good care),
knowing it held the secrets of birth.

* * * * *

They shook us and uttered most secular sounds.
"Pricks, prickles, thistles," they called to be mean,
sounds of damnation that vibrated down
to our roots and beyond where we wanted to be.
They kicked us farewell every dusk when the sun
had itself given rest to our stems and our leaves.
Then quickly they went to the inn just for fun,
safe from the highway robbers and thieves.
It happened one day a new monk arrived
in our garden by now a bed more than dry.
He'd small hands and feet, and a digging technique
different from any we'd known before, and
gently he'd urge us, gently he'd speak,
ask us to taste of a rich, fertile land.

* * * * *

We budded, we blossomed, our leaves turned from brown
to a green of no peer, so verdantly green.
We swayed in the breezes and danced up and down,
laughed in the sprays of the fountain and heat.
This was the change we sorely were needing.
Like bells we tolled, like carillon rang.
We loved Brother Martin and fruited seedlings.
Gratias agimus tibi we sang.
We fear one day he'll stay out of the glen.
We'll dry up and sharpen our needles again.
There'll be no explaining, no new green thumb.
The monks will fear blood drawn from their fingers.
"Pricks, prickles, thistles" will twist on their tongues,
while they hit us and stomp us in wild anger.

· Wednesday, October 4, 1021 ·

Bronwyn Reveals What Happened

One night this past August—I was 14½—
a soldier found me in one of my happy states
of calm after my father had gone to bed.

The handsome soldier took me in his arms,
and I could feel every cell within me open,
until each one was perfectly and fully blossoming.

I knew my mother would punish me severely,
most likely flog me, deny me food,
when she found out—and she did find out—

what I'd done that night with a guest.
And she has punished me over and over again,
for what I did with whoever he was.

I have refused to tell her the truth.

I'm sorry to say my father just whimpers
by himself in the toolshed. He never stays up
to joke with me anymore, before he closes the Song.

· *Tuesday, March 27, 1022* ·

Bronwyn's Aria

Warped woman, I
colorful
desolate
become
mother.
Colorful
artichokes
turn
brown.
Colorful
me, warped woman.

· *Wednesday, May 23, 1022* ·

Father Ralph Receives Three Returning Vegetable Gardeners

Three gardeners came back yesterday
from working vegetables far away—

happy the artichokes rallied green
(not praising Martin for being on the scene).

They were laughing, winking, smiling so
they told me how they'd come to know

Monday a babe was born at the Song,
wailing, crying a cat-bird song.

They laughed at the cost of this new life.
The mother was not the Innkeeper's wife.

Their glee at the expense of this child born
to twisted Bronwyn on Monday morn

was more than I could tolerate.
They joked the girl had not obeyed

her mother's rules for transient visitors,
soldiers, gardeners (smirking), and fiddlers,

who'd engage a girl in dialog, stirring
her flesh, her lips, her juices blurring

the line between what's right and wrong.
With a guest she blurred them all night long.

· *Friday, May 25, 1022, 1:30 p.m.* ·

Father Ralph Receives the Innkeeper and His Wife

Bronwyn's mother without hesitation
knew who'd created the "infestation."

She told her man, "Put the baby in a sack."
He did. They left with it slung on his back.

The hour was early by the clock's iron bells,
as they walked the road to my office-cell.

With spirits glum and deader than dead
here is what the couple said:

> *Innkeeper:*
>> With bad tidings on our lips,
>> we kiss your ring, Father.
>> Delicate news it is.
>
> *Innkeeper's Wife:*
>> Brother Martin isn't the glabrous-chested,
>> glabrous-cheeked vegetable gardener
>> we thought he was.
>> He's planted a seed in the wrong place, Father.
>> Our poor and darling girl cries now
>> in her sleep, ruined by Brother Martin.
>
> *Innkeeper:*
>> What does a girl-child know of having a child?

On my desk, the Innkeeper placed the babe
wrapped in a gray moth-eaten cape.

He and his angry unpleasant dam
ignored the babe's cries for a taste of a dram

of milk. Too young he was for infant pap.
There was nary a bootie or warming cap.

"Here," said the woman. "Take this ingrate.
He's fussy, colicky, underweight.

Goodbye, you old monk, who caused a bad end.
We'll not ever see this child again."

· *Friday, May 25, 1022, 3:25 p.m.* ·

Father Ralph Grieves for Brother Martin

Because the vegetable gardens are far away,
the gardener-brothers at the inn do stay.

And that's where Brother Martin slept.
Oh why, oh why? I wish he'd kept

his privates under his cassock hidden,
secret and on no cue bidden.

Delicate Martin, so fragile, mild.
Good Lord, he fathered Bronwyn's child!

He's not the type, not a bird of prey
to bed a young girl at end of day.

The Innkeeper and his sour wife
have abandoned the baby boy for life,

leaving him in my untried care.
I curse Brother Martin for this affair.

I'll punish him, too, for his transgression.
I'll send him away with utmost discretion.

This man of such a gentle side—
I thought his manliness had died.

How could Martin, such an innocent,
get into this predicament?

· *Friday, May 25, 1022, 4:05 p.m.* ·

Father Ralph Summons Brother Martin

Four being the hour, a messenger's gone
to get Brother Martin to the close by dawn.

I've called the boy back from the vegetable gardens.
I have no intention of granting a pardon.

I'll call him in to my cloister cell—
him, unsuspecting of what I've to tell.

Meantime, the babe must need some care.
My knowledge of infants is less than rare.

Needs he a hat? Needs he some shoes?
What does he need to be amused?

Should he be held? Should he be bathed?
Will he get out of this unscathed?

Oh, what should I do, what should I do?
I'm desperate, scared, and ignorant, too.

But what was that? The baby cooed,
surely a sign to call for Ralou.

I've asked her to come without further ado.
One look at the babe, and she'll know what to do.

And that is how we'll get through the night,
waiting for Martin to come at first light.

· *Friday, May 25, 1022, 5:00 p.m.* ·

Ralou Knows What to Do

Here at the monastery,
I've worked for almost

fifteen years. I've sat
with a few monks

as they lay dying. I've helped
some in fever. I've seen

some fall in love. I've seen
some in ecstasy. I've overheard

their prayers. I've washed
their clothes and mopped

their floors. I've cooked
their groats and sewn

their cassocks. But mercy
upon us, never have I tended

an infant in this place.
Heaven knows, I've plenty

of my own at home, but never
have I seen a prettier sight within

these walls. Father Ralph won't
tell me who the child is

(I'd like to thrash those
who gave him away),

but I will clean him up,
dress him properly,

feed him properly,
and sing to him so that he

will sleep well tonight
in preparation for

his new life with Brother Martin.

· *Saturday, May 26, 1022, 7:30 a.m.* ·

Father Ralph Hands the Baby Over to Brother Martin

This morning, to the creature in my company,
Brother Martin reached out tenderly.

"This is your son," I told him plain.
"Take him and raise him as you can."

"Be gone," I said. "Away you'll stay."
So with the newborn he went his way,

and as he left, without reserve,
he said, "This is more than I deserve."

He smiled a smile, the widest of smiles,
left humming a tune to the newborn child.

But those who know of this tragedy—
Innkeeper, his wife, Martin, and me—

haven't asked what Bronwyn desires to see
become of her flesh, her progeny.

How is she feeling, asked of us none,
is she motherly, sad, and missing her son?

She, poor girl, has been left to despair,
a defective body in toxic air.

Confidentially I must utter this:
Brother Martin was a man of bliss

as he walked outside with the babe in his arms,
smiling broadly with lips that formed

a symbol of happiness beyond all words,
a smile beyond a flight of birds.

How in God's name is he so blest?—
He knows just how to find peace, I guess.

· *Saturday, May 26, 1022, 7:45 a.m.* ·

Martin Sets Off with the Infant

Unfamiliar thoughts
    I have inside me this morning.
An unfamiliar look I know
    I must have on my face.

But who could ever draw the face of a parent
    who is childless and has a child?
Who can ever draw the face of the child
    who comes to the childless parent?

I will call him Dino.

Holding him and walking through the gates,
    I leave the close for the last time.

Ralou has sent this infant off with clean clothes,
    a new blanket, and a small vessel of milk.

She slept next to the child last night
    and told me he will be a good man.

She sneered, as she mumbled something about
    the contemptible deed of those who discarded him.

Who could do that? she asked. Who
    could give away their own flesh and blood?

She said she will pray for me as the child's father.
    She called me Brother Martin,

though she seemed to know something more
    about me. I am not a monk and never was.

I am this child's father now. I am this child's mother.

Through me his mother will exist, she'll hold him,
    nudge him, push the hair out of his eyes.

And he will call me Papa.

· Saturday, May 26, 1022, 10:20 p.m. ·

Father Ralph Reconsiders His Career

As abbot at the monastery
where atmosphere is light and airy,

I'm leader of a band of celibates.
I practice what I preach, no doubt of it.

Brother Martin was anomaly.
Strange, he had no beard to see.

His father gone, I sent him to
the vegetable gardens with the crew

of vegetable gardeners, a big mistake.
I'm the culprit. I'm the snake.

'Twas my decision to dispatch
the grieving boy to the garden patch.

In retrospect, I must declare
I never should've sent him there.

But it's too late to rue the day
I joined the brotherhood. I'll say

that once I'm buried in soil deep,
peaceful in my final sleep,

and once I'm there where angels sit,
I'll speak the truth, I'll tell, admit

I'm successful at creative,
not what's called administrative.

· Saturday, May 26, 1022, 10:37 p.m. ·

Martin's First Day as a Parent

I've brought my infant to the Sentry House
where there is no sentry, but where Father Ralph

arranged for us to live. It's night now. Incredulous
I am that such a day has come to me of barren womb.

What is one to do on the first day of being a parent?
No day in the calendar deserves more festival—

or sleep. For I am tired from the walk, but happier
than I've been all these fatherless days.

On the way here, I found a cow that gave us milk,
enough for both of us. We will sleep well tonight,

Dino and I, here, away from the brothers and the close,
beyond the reach of holiness, which mended and unmended me

and is forgotten here before the face of infant innocence.

· *Thursday, May 31, 1022* ·

Martin is a Mother/Father

On that first night in the Sentry House,
just a few days ago, I lay in bed,
listening for breathing sounds,
those puffs of air exhaled
from deep inside a little body,
sounds that belie age and size.
I do it still. I steal
next to the cradle to watch
for the heaving of Dino's chest
and shoulders. I sing to him.
I look at him
as if there's never been
a time since Creation
that either one of us existed
without the other.
Look on me, your father, I whisper,
look on me, your mother.
Dino will grow up safely
with the woman he calls father,
and I promise myself
that he will flourish in my care.

· Wednesday, October 19, 2022 ·

Mother Martina Is Aware of the Sainthood Campaign

There's a campaign afoot to make me a saint. Why now?
Well, I can't pretend that I haven't thought about it myself.

Today a rich man came by special boat to the island.
Shifts come about with circumstances.

Through the transparency of my coffin, I saw him
enter the chapel. Gold disks held the cuffs

of his sleeves together. His black coat was
of pure wool with a velvet collar.

The old woman Ralou, who tends to candles here
and sometimes sweeps the floor

and wipes clean the glass around me,
handed the man a Martin/Martina Society brochure.

He said to Ralou, with a toss of his head at me,
"Gotta get two miracles under his or her belt."

· *Monday, October 31, 2022* ·

Mother Martina Alone at Night Thinks About Sainthood

Becoming a saint
is close to impossible.
It takes money. I have none.
It takes friends. I have Ralou.
It takes centuries. I have those.
It takes societies and clubs. I've heard there is one.
It takes miracles. I have lived a miracle. I raised a child.
I was a child's father, and that's what put me
in this brocade gown and into this chapel.
I was his mother.
I was his father/mother.
That's a miracle in itself.
I could be a saint, couldn't I?
Ralou says I could.

· *Sunday, June 1, 1029* ·

Dino, Aged 7, Asks His Father for a Puppy

Papa, can I have a sister?

> *No, child, that won't be possible.*

Then, Papa, can I have a brother?

> *No, dear child, that too is impossible.*

What does impossible mean, Papa?

> *Well, I suppose impossible means questions, questions without satisfying answers. Impossible means dreams and wishes. Impossible means miracles, rainbows and crossed fingers.*

So, is it impossible for me to get a mother?

> *Yes, it's impossible.*

But what's not impossible is what's possible, isn't it?

> *That's a riddle, Dino.*

Look, Papa, my fingers are crossed.
Can I have a puppy?

· *Thursday, November 10, 2022* ·

Mother Martina's First Posthumous Miracle

The Martin/Martina Society's been
documenting my miracles. Dino's life
is the essence of miracle, but it is not
the drama islanders want to celebrate.

A recent afternoon, light of unusual
hue came high through a small chapel window,
and I sensed phenomenon at hand, mystery
causing all shadow to be purple.

A luminescence it was, prefix to a remarkable
event. When Ralou came in to extinguish
the candles, she said the sun was bright,
and a purple shadow made by the campanile

had moved across the façade of the opposite building,
one in need of paint. Ralou said she could see
the layers of aqua, blue, and terra cotta. She followed
the purple shadow as it settled, and she saw

my face in the rough texture of the stucco.
She cried out in the language of ecstasy,
though she was unable to repeat the sound for me.
Coffee drinkers looked up, she said, and fell

to their knees. The sun continued to shine
for fifteen minutes, and the face-shadow continued
to look out onto the square. It was my face,
the face of Dino's father, a woman named Martin/Martina.

That is my first miracle (or second after my boy).

That's how miracles happen. Constable Aldo,

who aspires to the job of mayor, took photos
to be uploaded into the ether proclaiming
that Mother Martina has made herself known

on the wall of an island building. Perhaps,
canonization *is* in my future. The rich man
who visited me here at my coffin has deposited
a large check into the Society's bank account.

· Sunday, November 13, 2022 ·

Mother Martina Focuses on Gender

I was a woman.
I was a man.
I was a woman.
I remained a woman.
I liked being a man.
I was a woman/man.

*   *   *

You might say I was masquerading.
That's not the right word. *Masquerade*
contains deceit. I did it for good reason—

I dressed as a man to stay with my father,
then for my father's memory,
then for Father Ralph, and to protect

a son, who knew me only as his father.
Others with whom our life connected
knew me, too, as Dino's father.

I was every bit as real in a man's cloth
as I could have been in a woman's.
I did it for myself as well, for my happiness.

Must that be called "living a lie"?
My heart was true, and I knew
I would be Dino's father forever.

I could have taken a wife into my bed.
I could have been the wife in my bed.
I could have found a husband in my bed.

But my energies went into raising
my son. I contained myself, a woman,
in bed with me, a man.

I always knew it would be like that.

· *Tuesday, January 10, 2023* ·

Mother Martina Remembers Raising Dino

Of course, we got a dog.
Dino loved Clint, who joined
us in the Sentry House,
a place of doors and walls
and stairs and shutters
and splinters in the floors
that found their way into Dino's knees—
when on all fours he crawled
and in his feet when he walked.

Dino loved Clint, as his brother,
a small ball of black curls.
Dino loved me, too, of that I am sure.

I continued to wear a cassock.
I feared the authorities would take Dino
away from me, if they found me
to be something other than
what they thought I should be.
People knew me as Martin.
Father Ralph took a liking to Dino
and saw that we had food and clothing,
and he taught Dino his letters and numbers.
He visited us frequently bringing
food and wine from the monastery:
carrots, potatoes, and lemons from the garden
but no artichokes. They had dried up,
he said, dried up mysteriously,
according to the gardeners.
We lived happily, Dino, Clint, and I.

· *Thursday, February 14, 1034* ·

Martin Explains to Dino, Not Quite 12

Dino, my boy, I have something to tell you.

> *What is it, Father?*

I am not your real father.

> *What?*

I am not a father at all.

> *But you're my father.*

No, I am not.

> *What?*

I'm not exactly a man.

> *Are you my mother then?*

No, I am not your mother.

> *Then who are you?*

I am Martin/Martina.

> *No, you are Martin my father.*

And I will continue to be Martin your father
but I wanted you to know the truth,

or at least the other side of it, so that
when I die and you prepare my body for burial,

you will not be surprised at what you see.

· *Friday, February 15, 1034* ·

Dino Absorbs What He Has Learned

I am a son of no one.
I am an orphan,
brother to a dog.
We are both motherless.
We are both fatherless,
and yet I have a father
who is a sort of woman
who is not my mother.
When I used to ask him
who my mother was,
my father would tell me
she was sick with disease
that ravaged her body,
so that she hunched over
and shuffled on twisted feet
until she could walk no further.
I have a father
who is a sort of woman
who is not my mother.
Their name is Martin.
Their name is Martina.
They are Martin/Martina.

· *Saturday, January 28, 2023* ·

Mother Martina Suspects She Has a Second Posthumous Miracle

The rich man's wife visited me last Saturday.
She knelt beside my glass coffin and spoke,
as only a woman confides in a woman,
her voice quiet like a dove's cooing in the rafters.

Who hears not the sounds of a woman dispirited?
Ralou, who was polishing brass, stopped to listen, too.

"Martina, I am married to a crooked man.
He has embezzled from his company
and thrown his workers out.
He has ruined the lives of his employees.
He says the best of times to fire people
is a holiday. He has thrown them into chaos
and poverty on Happiness Day."

Tears welled up within my eyes, for what person
weeps not at the sight of a weeping woman?
Tears rolled down into my ears. Tears tumbled
onto the satin pillow beneath my head.

And as the steeple clock struck five,
a man who smelled of eel came in, shuffling
of despondency. The embezzler's wife
departed, hid low her face from him,
recognizing one of her husband's workers.

Leaning on my coffin, the eel-man said,
"Martina, I've been fired, rendered penniless.
The company is bankrupt. I am, I am . . ."
Then he saw my tears and backed away.
"Miracle! Miracle!" he screamed,

shaking with new energy. "The impossible
is possible! Mother Martina is crying tears!
Real tears! Her pillow's wet. She's feeling
the sadness of my ruin, my end."

I believe I'm going to cry again.
The steeple clock has just struck five.
The tears come at full strength.

Canonization is a possible impossibility.
Ralou cleaned furiously after the eel-man left,
but she had a smile on her old face.

· *Monday, January 30, 2023* ·

Mother Martina Remembers the Day a Visitor Arrived at the Sentry House

One morning in May,
I looked out of an upstairs window
in the Sentry House,
roosters quiet by then
but Clint barking at a figure,
an odd-shaped figure,
angular figure, lumpy figure,
swathed in black muslin,
moving slowly and irregularly toward the house.

It approached our door.
Dino was playing with used water
in a tub in the kitchen.
He had made a boat
out of a stale loaf of bread.

I heard the knocks, but upstairs
I was too far away to keep Dino
from answering the door.
There was not a sound of voices,
only a silence, unlike any I'd ever heard.

I stayed at the top of the stairs
and watched the figure in black
envelop my boy in what appeared to be
a sweet and kind and secure embrace.
Only when I saw a withered foot
beneath the hem of the muslin
did I know that Bronwyn
had come in search of her son.

· *Saturday, May 11, 1034, 10:55 a.m.* ·

Bronwyn Meets Dino, a Play

[After the embrace, the figure
in black muslin holds the boy at a distance
in order to see his face and torso.]

The Figure:
    You must be Dino.

[She pushes his hair back from his eyes.
Dino shakes his head, yes.]

    I am Bronwyn.

[The boy is speechless,
and then with hesitation speaks.]

Dino:
    If you are Bronwyn, you are my mother.

Bronwyn:
    I am your mother.
    I know Brother Martin is your father
    and you love him, and he is good to you.

[Dino shakes his head, yes.]

    I will not take you away from him.
    I want to live here with you and him.

[Martin, still on the stairs, moves not a muscle
but watches to see Dino's reaction to this news.]

[Dino takes his mother's hand and kisses it.
Martin can almost feel the kiss. Dino says nothing,
but there's an understanding from the open door
and on up the stairs that Bronwyn has come home.]

· Saturday, May 11, 1034, 8:40 p.m. ·

Dino Contemplates the News That He Has a Mother

My father is not my father
because they are a man/woman
who is not my mother or my father.
I am a boy-child
but is it possible
that I am a girl-child?
Bronwyn says she is my mother.
Perhaps they are my father.
I am still an orphan.
Perhaps I am not an orphan.
I will speak about that with Bronwyn.

· *Tuesday, January 17, 2023* ·

Mother Martina Reminisces Further about Bronwyn's Arrival

For many years, I was expecting Bronwyn
to appear. I remembered her as precocious.

I knew that such a child, who had suffered
an experience far beyond her understanding at 14

(namely, to have given birth to another human being,
and to have that creature taken from her)

would eventually pursue a truthful answer
to any of her questions. So, I can't say

I was surprised to see her that morning.
What *did* surprise me was my own reaction

to her very arrival at our door
and her unexpected request to live with Dino and me.

I was delighted.

Here was Dino's birth mother,
27 years old by then, who was proving

to my child, and hers, better than I ever could,
that the impossible was possible.

· Monday, May 13, 1034 ·

Dino Asks About His Father

Who is my father, Bronwyn?

> *Martin is your father. You know that.*

I think of Martin as my father,
but that does not make him my father.

> *That's all you need to know. The man*
> *who fathered you would never be the father you have.*

Who was the man who fathered me? Did he have a name?

> *He did. But I do not remember it.*

Did he have a job?

> *He did. He was an itinerant soldier.*

My father was a soldier?

> *Dino, Martin is your father.*
> *He loves you and shows you how much he loves you.*
> *A father who does not show love to his child*
> *is not a father. A soldier-father, a father who can kill,*
> *forgets he is a father.*

Did my real father kill?

> *Possibly.*

Did my real father sing?

> *I don't remember. But a father who does not sing*
> *to his child is not a real father.*

Did my real father know how to cook?

> *A father who does not feed his child is not a real father.*

Did my real father do good deeds?

> *A father who does not know right from wrong is not a real father.*

Was my real father kind?

> *A father who abandons his duty is not a real father.*
> *A father who has nothing of the mother in him*
> *is not a real father.*
> *Martin is your father, Dino,*
> *and you are lucky for that.*

· *Saturday, January 21, 2023* ·

Mother Martina Is Grateful to Bronwyn

Bronwyn contributed to our home
in ways I never could have anticipated.
Of course, she helped with parenting.

She was a parent after all. And I, the grateful
father. She loved Dino beyond measure,
and he took on a new sense of himself.

I felt truly fortunate to have such a fine
partner as Bronwyn in raising our boy.
I loved her as much as I loved her son.

She stayed with us year after year
and we watched Dino grow up into a good man,
a good husband, a good father.

For twenty-five years Bronwyn stayed with us
until a fever came over her, not unlike the plague
that had taken my own mother away from me.

Dino and I and his family remained healthy,
though it is hard to know why. There was disease
all around us. Bronwyn's absence was felt

every day. At every breakfast. At every dinner.
Often we went looking for her, to tell her
something, forgetting that she'd gone.

· *Sunday, January 22, 2023* ·

Mother Martina Thinks Back on the Day She Died

Only three years after Bronwyn died
did I succumb
to nothing but the stoppage of my heart.

Dino in the privacy of my bedroom
cried next to me.
His wife was downstairs with the children.

It was his job to prepare my body for burial.
He undressed me.
I had readied myself for this moment.

I had tried to ready him for this moment.
With scissors,
he cut my cassock off me for ease of disrobing.

I cannot forget the look on his face.
He saw
that I was primarily a woman.

And it's as if everything I'd told him that day
came into focus.
It all meant something to him now.

He understood that I was a woman
destined
to be a man, destined to be his father.

And he wept as if there were a mother in him,
and he spoke to me.
"Thank you, Father," he said. "Thank you."

He washed me and sent a message to the monastery
asking Father Ralph
to come immediately, which he did,

though "immediately" for an octogenarian
is a relative term
meaning some long hours hence.

The old monk looked on my naked body
on the bed
and in rhyme declared me to be holy.

The two men dressed me in fine clothes
that would bespeak
neither man nor woman.

Father Ralph arranged for a glass coffin
to be delivered
to the Sentry House. I was taken away and brought

to this chapel on this island where I have been
for almost a thousand years.
It matters not to me that I am called Mother Martina.

· Thursday, February 2, 2023 ·

Mother Martina Has the Requisites for Sainthood

During the last three weeks my miracles
have taken on a life of their own.
More pilgrims than ever have been looking
for the purple shadow in the square.
And more than ever have come to visit me in the chapel
to see my tears at five o'clock.

Sometimes I cry.
Sometimes I don't.

But I don't care about sainthood much anymore.
I'm waiting for the most important miracle of all—
just one more, a third, that won't seem like
a miracle to anyone but me.

· *Friday, February 10, 2023* ·

Mother Martina Hears the Good News, a Third Miracle

This afternoon, a man 40 years old or so
and a woman probably somewhere in her 50s—
that would be my guess, though she
perhaps appeared older than she was—
came into my chapel. I'd never seen them before.
Ralou told me the man was a magistrate.
He was tall, healthy, swarthy, handsome.

He knelt at my coffin, while she,
who seemed to labor to walk,
hobbled to light some candles.
She carried brilliant green artichoke stalks
and placed them on my glass coffin.
She had a lovely face, not unlike that of the man,
perhaps her brother. I could see
that her feet, though shod, were misshapen,
and she moved with difficulty from candle to candle.

The man and woman brought with them
a feeling of comfort such as I remember
from the Sentry House. It made me think
of the good times when our trio lived
in happy company, until the day
our Bronwyn's breath gave out.

The man knelt and looked at me.
"Hello, Papa," he said,
"I've come with some news."
"What news?" I asked,
but of course he didn't hear me.
I had not been called Papa
for almost a millennium,

and I delighted in hearing it pronounced.
Whoever comes to visit me accepts me as I am.
Some call me Mother Martina.
Some call me Martin/Martina.
Clearly this man felt reverence for the father
I had been. The woman moved
with difficulty to join the man
at the side of my coffin, saying,
"Give your father the news, my boy."

The man then pulled his shoulders back
and set his jaw as he placed a hand
on the artichokes. And in the voice tone
of a magistrate, or a town crier, he addressed me
as Mother Martina, declaring that I would become
a saint within the next three years,
that I had accomplished the requisite
two miracles. That there was only
paperwork and bureaucracy, to finish off
the process and the ritual.

But I knew that a third miracle was happening
before my eyes and that messengers
had been sent to me from a thousand years ago,
and that something magnificent had happened
without acknowledgment from any maker of saints.

Ralou looked on, listening to what was happening.
She put the artichokes in a tall blue vase
and stood them next to my coffin.

It was 5 o'clock.

I watched the two visitors leave.
Tears filled my eyes and swam down my cheeks
and into the smile on my lips, and so I slept,
having seen my beloved son and Bronwyn again.

·Wednesday, February 17, 2027·

EPILOGUE: Ralou Mops the Floor of the Chapel

Well, she made it. I knew she would.
Saint Martin/Martina of the Anghinar.

They've taken her away from here
to install her in a cathedral.

I don't know where. It is lonely here.
I have no one to talk to. No glass coffin to polish.

No need for brochures, no visitors.
No brown and wilted flowers to throw away.

Still, I come to mop the floor every day
at five o'clock. And often as I mop, I cry.

St. Martin/Martina of the Anghinar.
I don't know where they got that name.

It's a mystery to me, but there was always
a lot of mystery about Mother Martina.

Mystery comes with secrets. She had
one big secret for a long time.

Mystery comes with hidden truths, too,
which might be called omissions.

Some might call omissions lies.
We all omit facts about our lives, I guess,

things we don't want others to know.
Holding the truth back causes pain

and frustration. I don't want anyone
to know that I still have

the artichoke stalks brought by the man
who told Mother Martina the good news.

I heard him call her Papa. And I smiled
because I knew how happy that made her.

We all like reminders of our past, things
that reconfirm that we lived once,

were young, were part of another combination
of space and time, people and home.

The artichoke stalks came into the chapel
a brilliant green, beautiful in the blue vase,

curly and joyous, almost laughing.
In a few days they were dried up

and beige, though still with an aura
of happiness. I couldn't bring myself

to dispose of them, so I took them home
and put them over my doorway,

where they are a symbol of the goodness
and kindness people are capable of.

They endure, even in the worst of times,
when plague ravages the world,

when sun heats the surface of the earth
to a burning point, when wind and rain

wash out all gardens, trees fall,
mudslides kill and destroy dwellings.

So, now I have told you my secret.
I feel better to have spoken it.

I will miss Mother Martina,
but I will always have her artichokes.

AFTERMATH

AUTHOR'S NOTE,
Aftermath

This novella in verse begins with a description of the catastrophe that has destroyed civilization. Weather events, disease, weapons, financial collapse cause widespread death, not only of peoples of the earth, but of animals and vegetation, including crops. But a few mighty trees have endured. The sun still shines.

And in a remote outpost, a band of survivors has thrived through ensuing centuries. The Weavers are the female survivors, the Fennel Men the males. The Builders are of a gender neither female nor male, and they cannot reproduce.

CAST OF CHARACTERS
· in order of their appearance ·

Fennel Men

Weavers

Builders

Wroc, a Weaver

Tris, a Builder

Dying Weaver

Tadz, son of Tris

Destruction
in which we learn of the aftermath of cataclysm

Just how it started—it is hard to tell:
some viruses, tornadoes, and some guns
did kill. And bombs of vengeful nations fell.

Constructions all of stone that weighed in tons
crumbled inches' fractions every day.
So schools and libraries closed down one by one.

Ionic columns—how they crashed and splayed
from every bank on every central street.
And corporations folded. Forgotten names,

numbers rotted: forty trillion beans.
Sheep's hair grew by inches, never shorn
'til beasts not eaten crouched upon their knees

and stopped their breathing, leaving bone and horn
and curly wool in clumps along the ground
just like coyote scat mixed up with corn.

A million ninety Guernseys wandered down
from their stanchions toward the orchard. Ten
billion smut-apples caused bovine wounds.

Windows of cars were broken with the intense
force of crowbars. Wallets vanished filled
with numbered dirty scrip and rubles, yen,

the last possessions of those who'd be fulfilled
with figures on paper only, which it was,
desiccating into lint and frill.

The rhododendron leaves were crisp because
the climate was so hot they didn't roll
like good cigars. Acorn pipes in jaws

disintegrated, new ones never sold.
There was no fire other than the sun,
for lighting up the story to be told.

Food was absent, no more bread or bun,
lettuce, kale, and spinach lost for good.
The kudzu leaf became the tasty one.

Survivors moved to beaches or to trees,
or else they lived in stacked and hut-like dens.
They loosely separated into three.

The Weavers lived with Builders in the huts,
but little time together did they spend.
The Fennel Men on the beach ate nuts.

These humans owned a personal self-sense
of how each fit within this three-part nation
of Weavers, Builders, and of Fennel Men.

The three groups knew by heart their obligations.
They got on well, one with both the others,
and worked at keeping sacred separations,

save when Weavers were longing to be mothers,
and wandered to the beach in search of fennel,
source of something more for them than brothers.

The Fennel Men
in which we meet the men who lived in trees on the beach

The Fennel Men did little but
sit in trees while with a knife,
they whittled awaiting death, and life.

Sometimes they walked on nearby roofs
of huts in search of Weavers' cloth.
Or, to find some love aloft.

Sometimes they walked along the shore
to gather something for supper's feed,
avoiding Builders stringing beads.

And as they walked the water's edge,
some felt their lungs not taking air.
But natural death brought no despair.

Most Fennel Men would sit in branches
and gargle among themselves non-words
about the unseen and unheard.

Long ago they might be called,
"good at heart," these Fennel Men,
kind and idle gentlemen.

Around their tawny sackcloth tunics
was tied an ecru sisal thong
slung on their hips low and long

and to it in a pale green hue
was a fennel bulb attached with twine.
The bulb reached down on the nimble line

above the knees between their thighs,
below the weave of their tunic hem.
Their circle—touching elbows, trim

angular frames, that met each other—
remembered without knowing why.
They whispered sounds both brown and shy

in memory: *Maman, swich licour,*
distant sounds—a *ferthyng* of grease
and crackle now. Girths, no increase.

Slight they were and ungues split.
Fur on their heads was parted sloppy
with curd-aroma and seed of poppy.

The Weavers and Their Cloth
*in which we meet the women who wove cloth for themselves
and the others*

Delicate were the Weavers' features.
Agile, graceful were these creatures.

Their skin was taut, a taupish rye,
their tawny braids reached their thighs.

Hopsacking skirts they cut and sewed
were dung-brown drab from waist to toe.

They wove the cloth the Builders' sewed—
tarpaulins for construction loads.

They wove the cloth for tunics, too,
that Fennel Men made from their high-tree view,

poorly pieced with edges rough.
What Fennel Men sewed was coarse and tough.

They weren't adept with the brittle needles
made from the horn of long-horned beetles.

The Builders
*in which we meet the beings who built houses for themselves
and the Weavers, one house atop the other*

The Builders all had varied looks. Some were strong,
with wide-spread hands, and dark hair plaited long.

The Builders lived in peace within each other's grace.
Some wore thread-bare chaps, some wore lace

over their sackcloth hand-sewn trousers. And they snuggled
one against the other in a huddle.

Sounds came forth from their ruby tongues like *shepe's woll*,
ancient memory of untranslated recall

that arose like cud in their throats to chew. And it was strange
that unknown sounds from long ago arranged

themselves in lines of unfamiliar noise. No need—
these fierce enormous Builders—no need to heed

those sleeping in the shoreline trees, the Fennel Men,
though on occasion they encountered them

on the beach where they, the Builders, often broke
routine to string some beads. Oh no, they spoke

at leisure times, Fennel Men and Builders, too.
They got along apart, as strangers do.

Builders built the high-stacked homes that they did share
with Weavers, though the two groups never paired.

Builders had no interest in sex or coupling,
though they were not averse to sometimes cuddling.

With Weavers they conversed in old and cryptic words
that came to them in sudden mystery conjured.

Weavers and Builders Together
in which we study two constituents of the three-pronged order

Where hardened Fennel Men went by Him's and He's,
Builders were They's, Weavers Her's and She's.

Between the She's and They's distrust was sown.
Together they lived—only from dusk to dawn.

The Builders had no possibility
of progeny, yet they quite typically

shared a common universal gender.
Some were rough and crude, others tender.

One might show attractive comely grace,
another would be callused, heavy-paced.

All Builders played the beads, it was their sport.
It satisfied their motive to resort

to competition, one against the other.
Who'd string the longest? Who'd be first to wither?

When they worked, the Builders nailed and sawed,
while Weavers fashioned cloth on looms as taught,

sitting steadfast in the weaving room—
each with loving care toward her own loom.

At times, some Weavers wandered off, perhaps
in search of those with fennel bulbs in laps.

At times, the Weavers felt an aching gut
like a dog in heat, perhaps a deer in rut.

Memory of Language
*in which we learn that ancient words came out of
Builders' mouths unexpectedly*

The Builders never found themselves content
to voice their feelings plain or to lament.

>   *. . . eche of other blother
the tone agayne the tother . . .*

Sounds like these would strangely emanate
from Builders' throats, secreted verbal state

that somehow reached back into memory
of feeling *moughte-eaten* since the year

when strong the vaults with crass excessive treasure,
wealth obscene beyond all worldly measure

collapsed into the rivers, broken streets,
this three-pronged order now left obsolete:

isolated Fennel Men so doomed,
Builders of homes, Weavers at their looms.

Memory of Sights
*in which pictures presented themselves in the mind
of the Weaver called Wroc*

While Builders secreted ancient language rimes,
some Weavers pictured scenes within their minds.

In their collective memories, they saw
creatures, not unlike themselves at all,

with four limbs and walking on hands and feet
and covered with white unruly hair, or neat.

Disbelief of such a creaturely line
made Weavers laugh, as they wove agave twine.

Sometimes their giggles were no more than a bleat
that made their laughter even more complete,

as memory sputtered like unexpected rain,
insidious, mocking showers on the brain.

Their laughter was a baa, a baa and baying,
'til Weaver Wroc left her bench, relating

sounds, looking at clouds through the door in the ceiling.
Where have they gone? Wroc cried soundlessly, kneeling—

*the creatures that walked on fours, their feet, their hands,
and gave their hair for capes, also for blankets?*

A thunder of bellow became a lively reminder,
a memory in sound, a hint of things lost but finer.

This Wroc, she shouted to wake the world from sleep:
Sheep! *Sheep*! The word is *Sheep*. It's *sheep*!

The others looked baffled. What words, oh Wroc, were these?
Poor sister Wroc, poor Wroc, had she been seized?

Building
in which we learn how the cluster houses, one atop the other,
were constructed

A Builder each morning would go to the flats,
needing some soil to make mud bricks—
with which They'd build another place,
safe from pollen, leaves, and sticks,
and air that made the breathing hard.

In the cluster of houses, the Builder, They,
three perfect sturdy walls would fix
to form a home of mud and hay
against an existing wall. And They
would set a roof of logs overhead
with a door cut in from a rooftop road.
For Builders and Weavers, a new homestead.

This road on high unmowed, unhoed,
was taken by all at different times,
Weavers and Builders. And as we'll see,
Fennel Men, too, climbed up on the road,
doing whatever would keep them free
of work and any responsibility.

With wood left over from making the roofs
the Builders built replacements of
the Weavers' aging wooden looms.
The Fennel Men, hiding possessions shoved
in holes, always kept to themselves,
not like what Weavers and Builders did.
But on occasion they climbed above,
up to the roof-road, for cloth amid
the Weaver's wares on which to bid.

Or more, perhaps, they climbed with hope.
That's how the Fennel Men would cope!

Expulsion, the Beginning of Disintegration
in which Tris went into labor, and the Builders prepared to execute Them

Early one morning, after the Weavers had gone to the looms,
a figure among the Builders—they called Them Tris—seemed
    consumed.

Tris hugged Themself and They breathed a halting noisy breath,
and the Builders not working, hearing this noise—those who
    were left—

were shocked and afraid as they did their daily chores in the house,
for the sounds they heard, the feral sounds that came out of
    the mouth

of Tris, a noise among Builders that no one had ever heard,
cries and moans, groans, unrecognized unknown words

up to when water flowed out of Them, who shouted out—
first, the sound *jesus,* then sounds of *jesus christ the lout.*

Sometimes, *jesus* and *fennel* gushed out as if one sound.
And the Builders dismayed looked blankly down at the arid ground.

Perhaps, they thought, one of the sounds, a word, or a gist,
was directed straight at a Fennel Man in their nearby midst.

But what would a Builder, who worked with wood, bricks,
    and more,
have to do with a Fennel Man, who lived in trees at the shore?

Not being a Weaver, how would a purposeful Builder react
to this incomprehensible, very mysterious fact?

And how could a Builder like Them have gotten plainly so near
to learn of Fennel Men's ancient names, or even to hear?

And what kind of names were these—an improbability?
The Builders then stopped to contemplate impossibility.

"Jesus" and "Christ" and what about "Christ the Lout"—such names?
Why was Tris screaming these words? Was Tris in some kind of pain?

Tris was in pain. Tris was squatting now to expel
something small. An unknown version of a Builder self.

The Builders knew enough to keep such secrets from Weavers.
They knew that they must locate the perpetrator-deceiver.

The Builders knew they had to dispose of Tris and the thing
in Tris's arms, to which they heard Tris sweetly sing.

Quick, dig a hole, cried the Builders at once, *a hole in the floor.*
They had in memory that such a thing had happened before

the treasure was lost. They knew what had to be done, and prepared
for burial. They dug, they dug until ancient words were aired—

> *Wepying and waylyng, care and oother sorwe*
> *I knowe ynough, on even and a-morwe*

Wooden T's, crosses, icons. They scowled in vain
at their cloth-covered feet. Their surprise, hatred, contempt was plain

for this *jesus*, this *christ*, this *lout*—the thing that did cause this pain.

Escape
in which Tris managed to escape burial in the floor

The Builders dug a hole in the floor for two,
for the Builder Tris and what They expelled,
which, by the way— it was not hard to tell—
had a fennel seed stuck to one of its toes.

As uncommon sounds from the little thing burst,
the others were digging. And Tris alarmed
with the curled-up thing in the crook of Their arm,
ran up the ladder to escape first

before fellow-Builders could take Them alive.
Tris with the little thing, wondrous gift,
flew through the woods, through the thickest mist
of salt and lea, like a bee from a hive.

Tris took the infant to the side of the sea
where nine months ago, at a beautiful hour,
a Fennel Man had offered a flower
to the Builder, who smiled tenderly.

And she—for Tris was a She to be called—
knew her behavior was thoughtlessly aberrant.
No longer a Builder it was apparent,
but neither was she a Weaver at all.

Dying at a Loom in the Weaving Room
in which Wroc the Weaver knew just what to do

A Weaver at her loom precariously slumped
making some sounds—unknown the intent—
slid off her bench with a terrible thump.
Almost finished, the sackcloth length,

she said. And under the bench she lay,
as her breath's rhythm fairly diminished,
and her face was smudged from the floor of clay.
My sackcloth length is almost finished,

she mumbled and slurred. Wroc came close,
held her, who cried of *cloth* and *sack*
and *length* until she no more spoke
weaver-sounds, as her world turned black.

Is the sackcloth finished at the silent loom almost?
asked other Weavers getting sadder and sadder
for the now-dead, voiceless Weaver-ghost,
whom Wroc then carried up the ladder.

A young Weaver waiting up on the roof
for such a sign to begin her descent,
exchanged her place with Wroc on a rung
and each then moved to where she was meant.

The young one, the novice, went down to the room
where she listened to others chanting the sounds
sack-cloth-finished-silent-the-loom,
which told her just where her work would be found.

Burial of a Weaver

in which Wroc carried the dead Weaver's body to the hut she shared with the Builders

Wroc took the corpse to the dead one's house,
over the roof-road up to the door.
Who would be there at this odd morning hour?
Likely some Builders, three, four, or more.

They sat together eating pears with brew
when Wroc with the body on the ladder came down.
The Builders, who'd known just what to do:
dig a hole in the floor of dusty packed ground.

Of course, the hole was already dug,
but a purposeful digging the Builders feigned,
shielding it partly by the sisal rug
so that Wroc the Weaver would not ascertain

that one of the Builders had disappeared,
in fact, had become as *She* as a Weaver,
had produced a thing with a fennel seed
that clearly and truly would never leave her.

A Builder washed the dead Weaver and put
a pear slice wrapped in an aspen leaf
between the toes of each pretty foot—
singing a song of remembered belief.

> *Dona eis requiem*
> *To plesen hem*
> *I wol do my labour*
> *Amen Amen Amen Amen*

They put her into the grave They'd dug—
dug in the floor of the house where Tris
had betrayed with collective memory's tug
running out of the house into Fennel Man's midst.

Then the Builders left to compete at stringing
beads, their sport, where another team waited.
After a morning of ritual singing,
they needed to relax with beads they braided.

Weaver Wroc, up and down climbed
ladders, going back to the weaving room,
where the strange sounds had already died
and the novice was weaving cloth on the loom.

Stringing Beads for Relaxation
*in which the Builders came across an indistinguishable carcass
on the beach*

Seagulls, flying low, proclaimed to the Builders
that a carcass was now on the beach. Bewildered
they sniffed a putrid smell. The sun
was hot. And after what Tris had done—

not being a Builder, not what they'd thought—
and after the Weaver whose heart had stopped—
they knew they needed a change in their day,
some kind of fun without delay.

So they went to relax, to string beads that they'd wear
around their necks, or in their hair.
Teams would compete for the pieces of bone
that they found on the beach, though never a stone.

But there was a carcass. Had it been killed?
Had it walked on two feet? did it weave? Did it build?
Did a fennel bulb dangle between its thighs?
Did it understand memories behind its eyes?

The two Builder teams were sitting aground,
beading seeds on twine they had already wound,
giving each seed the name of a thought
of something past like a lesson taught.

Meanwhile, gulls in formation came near
and drew a line deep and sharply clear
with their talons across the sand. They began
to tear at the flesh's succulent glands.

Both teams watched, fingering beads,
up to the crushing of fennel seeds.
Each Builder heard the gull-made noise
on a skeleton showing up, picked-clean poised.

And they all recognized their very own frame,
as if Builder and Fennel Man were one and the same.
They knew the bones would bleach chalky with time
void of their yellow-green putrid slime.

They'd cut the bones, make charms with holes,
fashion some bracelets or whatever they chose.
They'd string the charms, even bone from the skull,
then add beaks and talons and feathers of gull.

What they never found out, never could tell,
was where Tris went with the thing she'd expelled.
They didn't see that she'd stayed near the sea
or had found a safe place to live in a tree.

Truth was she'd hidden from Builders among
the good Fennel Men, who fed mother and young
Fennel Man babe, who would grow to be grand,
though his sire was gone, dead on the sand.

At Night at Home
in which Wroc sensed the absence of two creatures

Weavers returned to the house that night,
at first not seeing that Tris wasn't there.
Covered up, the burial hole in the floor,
where the dead Weaver lay under rug and chair.

Some of the Builders knew the truth,
the grave dug for Tris and the thing she'd expelled
(the grave that later embraced the Weaver
who'd died at her loom, sad to tell).

Wroc, who entertained ovine perceptions,
was nervous. In no way could she be stayed.
"Something's not here," she said, "one, maybe two—
as if a ewe and a lamb have strayed."

Distraught already from the death of the Weaver,
she looked at the rug, at the grave, and beyond.
Something was surely further amiss
not just the Weaver, but a Builder was gone,

Wroc began talking inside of her head.
Is there more than one body down in the hole?
I sense there is something not as I think it.
I sense a game's been played with some souls.

Spread out in bowls of vegetable broth
was the meal for the Builders and Weavers alike—
stewed leaves of kudzu and vines of the same,
some hard-boiled, while others were fried.

The Weavers looked down at the fare on the table,
looked all around at the faces unlit.
"Who could be missing?" "Are we all here?"
And in a voice firm, but edgy with grit,

Wroc cried, "That grave newly dug in the floor—
The hole was not made for the Weaver, I'm sure!
I sense, it's clear, one turned into two
and they've left our home without notice or word."

Proud of being neither female nor male,
the Builders resented the Weavers' questions.
And angry they were that Tris had escaped
to hide—who knew where?—her Builder transgression.

The Weavers were soundless in comfortless fright,
kept eyeing the kudzu that made up their meal.
Wroc raised her arms and spoke out above them:
"Our three-pronged order has broken its seal."

Distrust
in which the already loose tripartite band disbanded completely

The seeds of distrust in the world had been cast.
Wary of Fennel Men, Builders withdrew.
Wary of Builders, Weavers were through
with co-existence. The three groups did ask

to live separately, no contact at all.
Each group would learn the other's job.
They'd stick to themselves, no more hobnob,
and all three would shirk a community call.

Each group learned to weave and to build.
Each group stayed away one from the other.
Each learned to play at stringing beads, rather,
and each had its trees and each had its guild.

With one exception, the Fennel Men's band
now took Tris as part of the pack
(along with the little thing slung on her back).
Tris, ready with a helping hand.

All of these creatures, split into three,
kept their distance, six feet allowed,
but something was missing. *That* they avowed:
life was different with autonomy.

The Three Groups in Isolation
in which we see that the three packs were self-sufficient at work and play, and we meet Tadz

1
The Fennel Men often lived weeks at a time
in old empty houses built out of pine.

But arboreal action, they knew, wasn't done.
They went to the beach and climbed trees just for fun.

They learned to build houses—houses they stacked
one on another—and wove clothes they'd lacked.

Tris taught them how to use tools in their labor.
A valuable asset, she was their favored.

They learned construction, they learned how to weave
on looms that they built with wood from the trees.

They severed the fennel bulb hung from their waist,
once thought to give them prestigious place.

They cut it in pieces, strung it on string,
to wear from their neck. Tris too wore the thing.

2
The Weavers discovered for needed leisure
time could be spent in utmost pleasure

stringing beads, as Builders still strung.
Stringbone, they called it, a name to be sung.

They learned to construct, stack homes of their own
entered from high, since that's what they'd known.

The Weavers let Tris and her boy with them dwell
when they weren't with the Fennel Men, collecting shells.

The boy was a star. His name was Tadz,
T-A-D-Z, a gem among lads.

He worked with the Builders, knew how to weave,
was usually serious with plans up his sleeve.

3
The Builders were carpenters, handy with tools.
Where weavers once lived, they made sofas and stools.

They liked solitude, free of the mix.
They saved broken looms they knew how to fix.

They learned how to weave, how to gather wood pulp,
and for fun they fashioned a Fennel Man's bulb.

The Builders were pranksters, up to no good,
but all to annoy whomever they could.

The Next Generation
in which we meet the group of twelve and the force of DNA

Soon more creatures joined the young Tadz,
A happy dozen born playfully glad.

Twelve young things, not just of one kind—
Four came with fennel bulbs' familiar sign.

Four came with hammers and saws as clues,
each with a fennel seed hidden from view.

Four came with cloth like a caul of reeds,
and even they hid fennel seeds.

All twelve of them entered the Weavers' life
born naturally without aid of knife.

And so like Tadz, among Weavers they stayed,
learned how to walk, how to talk, how to say

the ancient words the Builders remembered
from Janus month all the way to December.

But those with the fennel bulbs at the age of three
joined their fathers in the shoreline trees.

Those with the saws of varying blades
moved in with Builders where they learned the trade

of erecting a house, a table, a loom,
and there they grew with plenty of room.

Those who were born with cloth did not leave
but stayed with their mothers and learned how to weave.

From a young age, the twelve found each other,
played without telling father or mother.

The twelve met secretly down on the beach
to play music or dance or in Stringbone compete.

A tight-knit group they did comprise
with Tadz, the oldest, considered most wise.

On Even Footing: The End and the Beginning

So naturally as life finds its end,
the elders died off, the Fennel Men,

the Builders, so too the generous Weavers,
leaving the twelve happy receivers

of talents and genes to do them good stead,
but all as one, like-minded, it's said.

There were others of course who came one at a time,
each taking the place of one who had died.

The new generations fostered no pique,
loved one another, the strong and the meek.

They built and they wove, and they lolled on the beach.
They learned by themselves what no one could teach.

Tadz spoke up when the elders were gone,
"Come now," he said. "What's done is done.

"It's time to get rid of our parents' factions
We all love each other, time to take actions."

So they worked and they played, all in together,
combined into unum, separate never.

They all had ideas. They all had habits.
Some lived in trees, some in cabins.

Memory came to some of them then
and not to others. They never knew when.

Some thought of fennel, some ate neeps.
Some had subconscious memory of sheep.

Some were better at building than others.
Some just wanted to be happy mothers.

Some looked ahead and cared not for lore.
Some knew the history and words of yore.

It was time to let pasts be as they are,
but they didn't forget what got them this far.

Together they built. Together they wove.
Life was a treasure that went beyond trove.

ACKNOWLEDGMENTS

Normally I would list here in gratitude the journals that included certain poems in this book, but by the very nature of these two novellas, no individual poems have been previously published. However, I want to thank those who—throughout the time I was working on these as well as other poems—gave me valuable support and encouragement: The Capitol Hill Poetry Group and the Chester Poets, both of whom have sustained me for many years; a group I call "Vicki Poetry" comprised of friends who just love poetry, originally hosted by the late poet Vicki Lambert; and two other groups that originated out of the Pandemic on Zoom: The Glow, founded by poet Hiram Larew; and Friday Lunchtime Poetry, hosted by poet Martin Vernon in Ennis, Co. Clare, Ireland. I owe a world of gratitude to two poet-friends who read the manuscripts of the novellas, Nancy FitzHugh Meneely and Patric Pepper. Of course, I am forever grateful for the love and kindness of my two children, Greg and Alexi Lalas, my two step-children, Sarah O'Keefe and Rick Woodworth, and their families. And I thank my four siblings for our monthly Zoom talks and their interest in my work.

ABOUT ATMOSPHERE PRESS

Atmosphere Press is an independent, full-service publisher for excellent books in all genres and for all audiences. Learn more about what we do at atmospherepress.com.

We encourage you to check out some of Atmosphere's latest releases, which are available at Amazon.com and via order from your local bookstore:

The Unsolvable Intrigue, poetry by D.C. Stoy

Words of a Feather Hawked Together, poetry by Linda Marie Hilton

I Am Not Young And I Will Die With This Car In My Garage, poetry by Blake Z. Rong

Love, Air, poetry by Lawdenmarc Decamora

To Let Myself Go, poetry by Kimberly Olivera Lainez

less on that later, poetry by Madeline Farber

The Last Hello: 99 Odes to the Body, poetry by Joe Numbers

Granddaughter of Dust, poetry by Laura Williams

Nest of Stars, poetry by Nicole Verrone

Damaged, poetry by Crystal Wells

I Would Tell You a Secret, poetry by Hayden Dansky

Aegis of Waves, poetry by Elder Gideon

Footnotes for a New Universe, by Richard A. Jones

Streetscapes, poetry by Martin Jon Porter

Feast, poetry by Alexandra Antonopoulos

River, Run! poetry by Caitlin Jackson

Mud Ajar, poetry by Hiram Larew

ABOUT THE AUTHOR

Anne Harding Woodworth is passionate about narrative, whether it's fiction, poetry, non-fiction, or a combination of any and all. *Gender* joins her seven other books of poetry, one of which, *Spare Parts*, is also a novella in verse. Her book *Trouble* received the 2022 William Meredith Award for Poetry. Harding Woodworth has lived in New Jersey, Michigan, and Athens, Greece, which have all contributed to her love of story. She and her husband now live in Washington, DC, where she is a member of the Poetry Board at the Folger Shakespeare Library. She also serves on the Board of Governors at the Emily Dickinson Museum, Amherst, MA.

Lightning Source UK Ltd.
Milton Keynes UK
UKHW010641291222
414571UK00004B/333